Once in a Blue Moon

By

NICOLA MORGAN

Toronto   Oxford   New York
OXFORD UNIVERSITY PRESS
1992

Oxford University Press, 70 Wynford Drive, Don Mills, Ontario, M3C 1J9

Toronto Oxford New York Delhi Bombay Calcutta Madras Karachi
Petaling Jaya Singapore Hong Kong Tokyo Nairobi Dar es Salaam
Cape Town Melbourne Auckland

and associated companies in
Berlin Ibadan

Canadian Cataloguing in Publication Data

Morgan, Nicola, 1959-
Once in a blue moon

ISBN 0-19-540831-4 (bound)   ISBN 0-19-540881-0 (pbk.)

I. Title.

PS8576.07305 1991   jC813'.54   C91-094751-1
PZ7.M670n 1991

Oxford is a trademark of Oxford University Press
1 2 3 4 - 5 4 3 2

Printed in Singapore

– For Wynn –

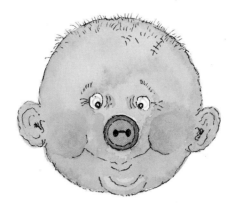

who is as cute as a button!

Aunt Floydie was as old as the hills and a little forgetful. But she was also big and strong and fit as a fiddle.

She lived alone in a small house
on the edge of a quiet town,
far, far away from the rat race.

Aunt Floydie had three very best friends.
There was the mailman, who came every day in his truck.
Aunt Floydie liked him
because he was always full of beans.

And then there was the Countess.
She had a fancy house, lived high off the hog
and was always dressed to the nines.

There was also the Mayor.
He was very jolly, though he often put his foot
in his mouth and ended up in quite a pickle.

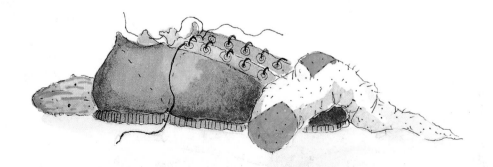

One morning Aunt Floydie woke up
and remembered it was her birthday.
She had forgotten to plan a party and she had
forgotten to tell her three best friends.
But worst of all, Aunt Floydie had forgotten
how old she was. She began to feel a little blue.

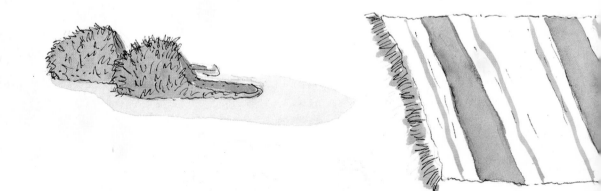

Aunt Floydie had quite a green thumb, so she
went out to the garden to work and think.
She clipped the roses and weeded the pansies.
She tied up the peas and thinned the carrots.
Soon she began to feel better.
She was as busy as a bee.

Aunt Floydie was so busy, in fact,
that she didn't even notice
a dark cloud in the sky.
It grew large and burst
right over the garden.
Before long it was raining
cats and dogs. By the time
she reached the house,
Aunt Floydie looked like
something the cat dragged in.

When Aunt Floydie stepped inside,
she could hardly believe her eyes.
There were her three
very best friends, the mailman,
the Countess and the Mayor.
On the table was a cake
fit for a king and it had
Aunt Floydie's name on it.

"Surprise!" they all shouted.
Aunt Floydie was tickled pink.

Then the mailman played the fiddle
and everyone danced up a storm.
The Countess sang until she had
a frog in her throat.
The Mayor gave a lovely toast.

The party was in full swing.

Nobody could remember how old Aunt Floydie was.
They thought and thought and they all
decided together that it really didn't matter a fig.

"What's important," said the mailman, "is that
you are as healthy as an ox . . ."

". . . and as happy as a lark . . ." added the Countess,

". . . and your heart," smiled the Mayor,
"is as big as all outdoors."

The party continued
until the cows came home.
Then the mailman, the Countess
and the Mayor all had to leave.
They each gave Aunt Floydie
a wonderful birthday hug
and slipped into the night.

Aunt Floydie smiled as she waved farewell.
"I may be as nutty as a fruitcake," she whispered,
"but my friends are as sweet as apple pie."

That night, Aunt Floydie was on cloud nine
as she drifted off to sleep. It had been
such a wonderful, magical day . . .
a day she would always remember . . .
a day that comes . . .

. . . Once in a Blue Moon.